By **Brooke Vitale**

Illustrated by **Paul Conrad** and the **Disney Storybook Art Team**

Designed by **Winnie Ho**

🏆 A GOLDEN BOOK • NEW YORK

Copyright © 2021 Disney Enterprises, Inc. All rights reserved. Published in the United States by Golden Books, an imprint of Random House Children's Books, a division of Penguin Random House LLC, 1745 Broadway, New York, NY 10019, and in Canada by Penguin Random House Canada Limited, Toronto, in conjunction with Disney Enterprises, Inc. Golden Books, A Golden Book, A Little Golden Book, the G colophon, and the distinctive gold spine are registered trademarks of Penguin Random House LLC.
rhcbooks.com
ISBN 978-0-7364-4078-3 (trade) — ISBN 978-0-7364-4079-0 (ebook)
Printed in the United States of America
10 9 8 7 6 5 4 3

I turn around at the **honk** of a horn and see a large boat headed our way. This is it! **THE JUNGLE CRUISE!**

Albert, the skipper, announces, "We begin our tour in the Amazon!"
We leave the dock.

"If you wonder how many birds can fit on one branch, it appears *tou*-can," he says.

I turn away in time to see a giant python **HISS** and lunge for Mom.

"Whew. Looks like that guy has a *crush* on you, huh?" Albert says.

Suddenly, water splashes up from the river.
"Watch out!" Albert exclaims. "Man-eating piranha! Women and children, don't worry. They're only *man*-eating."

We leave the piranhas behind.

"Now, please," Albert says, "if you're wearing yellow, don't make any **noises** like a banana . . . it drives him *ape*!"

"My camp's just up ahead,"
Albert explains. "I just— Oh boy. . . ."

OOH-OOH!

A band of gorillas is destroying the camp!

"Guys! I told you to break *camp*, not everything I own!" Albert shouts toward shore.

The boat pulls up next to a giant African bull elephant.
"Their great tusks make it easier for them to forage for
food, and to terrify our Jungle Cruise skippers!" Albert says.

We move down the river.

"Knock, knock," Albert says. "Who's there? Safari. Safari who? *Safari*, so good!"

GRRR.

HUFF.

HUFF.

Across the river, a rhino chases a group of explorers up a tree!

"Rule number one of the jungle: you can't outrun a rhino!" Albert says. "Don't worry. Those guys will get the *point*."

We look ahead again and see huge hippos rising out of the water.

"We are now turning in to a pool of **dangerous hippos**," Albert says. "Last week, they overturned six of our boats—only *five* of them were mine!"

As we slow down, Albert steers us under a waterfall.
"There it is, ladies and gentlemen, the Eighth Wonder
of the World—the **Backside of Water**! Don't try this
at home."

Nearby, I see something that looks like an ancient temple. "What could be inside these mysterious ruins?" Albert asks us. "Valuable riches? Eternal youth? *My last crew?* Let's find out!"

"Right, then," Albert says. "Let us proceed, shall we? Tigers are hard to *spot*. After all, they're striped!"

The boat emerges from the temple.

"Aww, look at those elephants bathing over there," Albert says.

"Duck! Duck!"
Mom shouts.
"No, ma'am.
Elephants, not ducks,"
replies Albert.

Finally, the boat reaches the dock.

"That concludes our tour," Albert says. "I hope you enjoyed your time aboard the world-famous **JUNGLE CRUISE!**"

"That ride was awesome!" I say. "Can we go again?"

"Great idea! I think I will . . . ," jokes Albert.